GIFT OF THE NILE

AN ANCIENT EGYPTIAN LEGEND

RETOLD BY JAN M. MIKE   ILLUSTRATED BY CHARLES REASONER

TROLL ASSOCIATES

I N THE TIME when Senefru was Pharaoh over all Egypt, a young girl named Mutemwia came to live in the Royal Palace. She was sent by her father as a present to Pharaoh so that she might gain his favor.

Mutemwia soon became a favorite among the women at the palace, for, though she had little beauty, the girl was kind and honest. Pharaoh's magician, Zajamunkhu, upon hearing of her, came to meet her himself. He listened as she played her harp and sang to entertain the other women.

GIFT OF THE NILE

Library of Congress Cataloging-in-Publication Data

Mike, Jan M.
  Gift of the Nile: an Ancient Egyptian legend / retold by Jan M.
Mike; illustrated by Charles Reasoner.
    p.   cm.—(Legends of the world)
    Summary: During a magical boat ride on the Nile, Mutemwia proves
that her love for the Pharaoh is a gift of the heart and needs no
cage to hold it.
  ISBN 0-8167-2813-5 (lib. bdg.) ISBN 0-8167-2814-3 (pbk.)
    [1. Folklore—Egypt.] I. Reasoner, Charles, ill. II. Title.
III. Series.
PZ8.1.M595Gi 1993
[398.2]—dc20   92-5826

As was his custom, Zajamunkhu ate dinner with Pharaoh Senefru that evening. As they dined, he spoke well of the girl, Mutemwia. Pharaoh had many cares and few people who might share them. So, he sent for Mutemwia, that her music might give him rest.

"Long life and health to you, great Pharaoh," Mutemwia said as she entered his room. Her voice was soft and low, and Pharaoh saw that the hand that held her harp trembled.

"Do not fear me, Mutemwia. I would have you play soft music and sing my cares away," Pharaoh said. He reclined upon his couch, and the music of Mutemwia brought him great comfort.

For many nights, Mutemwia came to play for Pharaoh, and soon she lost her fear and grew to care for him greatly. Her music brought them both great joy.

The days passed into weeks. It came to be that Pharaoh spoke to her of his worries and cares, and she listened and gave him good counsel. Each evening, Senefru and Mutemwia talked, until the moon was bright above the Nile.

Senefru learned that Mutemwia was both intelligent and honest. Though many people spoke only to please Pharaoh and said only what they thought he wished to hear, Mutemwia spoke the truth to him always.

One day, word of trouble came from a city in Pharaoh's realm. Senefru had to leave his court and travel for many days. Mutemwia was left to await his return.

When Pharaoh returned, he went to Mutemwia and found her thin and pale. Pharaoh sent for his cooks and ordered them to prepare special foods for Mutemwia.

"You must eat and grow strong, for though you missed me, I have returned," said Senefru as he fed her with his own hand.

"Long life and health to you, Pharaoh, but I cannot eat. It is true that I missed you, but I also miss my old life. I long for the river I once waded in and the hills I once climbed. This food, to my mouth, tastes like sand, and the air in this room is the air of a tomb. My Pharaoh, I cannot live my life in a cage, however beautiful that cage may be." Mutemwia spoke these words, though she feared they would offend Pharaoh, for they were true words.

ENEFRU grew angry. His pride was wounded at the thought that Mutemwia missed her freedom more than she had missed him. He drew himself up and left her room without speaking. For many nights after, Pharaoh remained alone.

He did not see Mutemwia. Nor did he give her her freedom, for he feared he would lose her forever if she were allowed to leave. In his private heart he feared he had already lost her.

The days grew hot and sticky. The sun was too bright. Flies buzzed about the palace courtyards. It seemed to Senefru that the people who surrounded him chattered like birds and spoke no more wisdom than the pigs of the farmer. Their games and diversions bored him.

INALLY, Pharaoh sent for Zajamunkhu. "My friend," he said to the magician, "food, to my mouth, tastes like sand, and the air in this palace is like the air of a tomb. The people who surround me chatter like birds, and they can think of no game to amuse their Pharaoh."

Zajamunkhu was a wise man. He knew of the great friendship between Senefru and Mutemwia. Though Pharaoh did not mention her name, Zajamunkhu knew what troubled Pharaoh's heart.

"Peace and long life to you, Pharaoh," he said. "If the air in here is as the air of a tomb, then go forth from the palace. Order a boat to carry you along the cool path of the Nile. Call forth twenty women to row for you. And set one woman above them to steer the boat and sing for you. Then may you see the birds that nest along the river, the green fields and grassy banks. Then may your heart find contentment."

"You are wise, Zajamunkhu. It shall be as you say."

Zajamunkhu ordered that a boat be brought, and that special oars be made of ebony and electrum. He had new clothes made for each of the women. And he ordered, for each woman, a flower of copper to adorn her hair.

For Mutemwia, who would steer the boat and sing, Pharaoh himself ordered a dress adorned with golden threads. And, for her hair, a golden lotus flower with a heart of blue lapis. These he brought to her when all had been made ready to sail.

Mutemwia gave a cry of joy at seeing Senefru, for she had missed him. As Pharaoh gave her his gifts, he said, "You cannot leave me, Mutemwia, for you are my most true and honest friend."

Gentle breezes blew over the Nile. The women who rowed the boat were strong and graceful. Mutemwia's voice was sweet to Pharaoh's ears as she steered the boat and sang.

Pharaoh saw the birds that nested along the Nile, the green fields, and the grassy banks. He saw Mutemwia's cheeks grow rosy in the warmth of the sun, and his heart was content.

So he might have remained, but a harsh wind rose up and took from Mutemwia's hair the golden lotus that Pharaoh had given her. Mutemwia stopped singing and cried out in dismay as she watched her flower sink beneath the surface of the Nile. Without her song to guide them, the women could not row, and the boat was stilled.

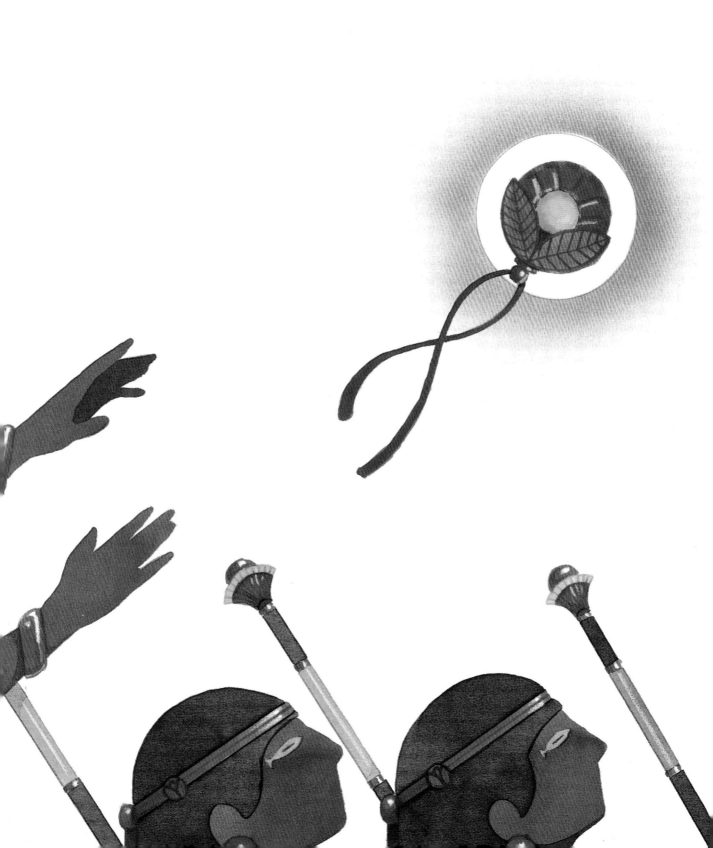

"Do not cry, Mutemwia. Only sing and steer the boat, and I will give you a hundred golden flowers when we return," Senefru called to her.

"Long life and health to you, Pharaoh. I do not want a hundred flowers, only the one that you gave me this day, when you told me I was your most true and honest friend."

Zajamunkhu saw that the women had ceased to row, and he grew concerned. He approached Pharaoh, and Senefru told him what had happened.

"Peace and long life to you, Pharaoh," said Zajamunkhu. "I will do what I can, and in truth it is no great magic to me."

Zajamunkhu spoke words of power, and the air grew thick with silence as the mighty Nile split down the middle, like a stone of granite under the tools of a mason. He lifted his staff, and lightning flashed forth from it, and, lo, half of the river rose into the air and lay itself atop the other half.

Pharaoh's boat drifted slowly through the air and came to rest on the dry river bed. Beside the boat the river loomed, so high it seemed to touch the very sky. Everyone was frightened to see the wall of water, held fast by nothing more than the magician's words. Even Pharaoh looked upon the wall of water in great wonderment and forgot all else.

 NLY ONE person paid no attention to the water. Mutemwia was neither frightened nor astonished. Along the dry river bed, she saw a flash of gold in the summer light. Swiftly, she climbed out of the boat and ran to get her golden lotus. Grasping it in her hand, she returned to the boat.

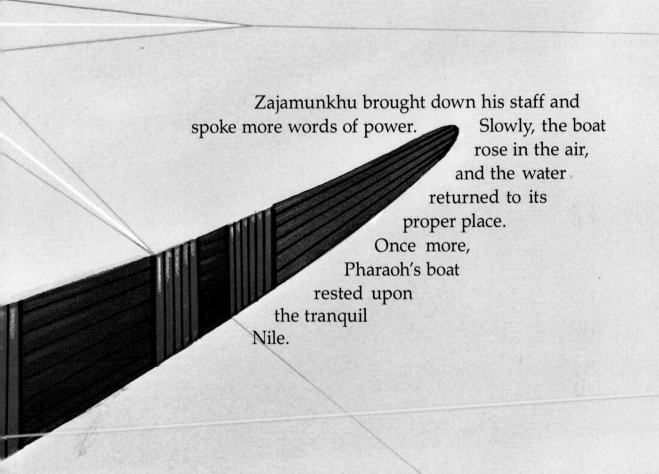

Zajamunkhu brought down his staff and spoke more words of power. Slowly, the boat rose in the air, and the water returned to its proper place. Once more, Pharaoh's boat rested upon the tranquil Nile.

Mutemwia turned to Senefru, and he saw that the love she held for him was true. Such friendship was a gift of the heart and needed no cage to hold it.

"This golden lotus, that you rescued, will forever be my pledge of love to you," said Pharaoh to Mutemwia. "I can see the friendship you hold for me. Therefore, I will give you your freedom and a house near the palace, and in this way we will be friends for many years."

So it came to be that Mutemwia left the Royal Palace and lived in her own house. Many people came to her for counsel and advice, and she prospered and grew rich as the years passed. To the end of her days she wore no other jewelry than the golden lotus of Senefru. And always she remained the most true and honest friend to Pharaoh.

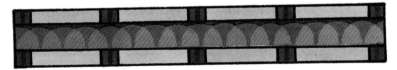

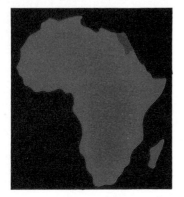

We know a great deal about ancient Egypt because of hieroglyphs. Hieroglyphs, or picture writing, were painted or carved on stone or drawn on paper made from the papyrus plant. *Gift of the Nile* comes from a papyrus hieroglyph that was written about 3,500 years ago.

The great Egyptian civilization grew along the fertile banks of the Nile River more than 5,000 years ago. The rulers of Egypt were called pharaohs. The Egyptians believed that the pharaoh was a special god put on earth. He owned the entire kingdom and all the people living in it. The pharaoh was to rule according to laws given to him by Maat, the goddess of truth and justice. This meant that he was to rule honestly and fairly.

Religion was very important in ancient Egypt. There were many gods. They had human and animal characteristics, as well as magical powers. Priests and magicians called on these powers to help the people with their fears. Magic explained many strange things that happened in nature, like the great uplifting of the river in *Gift of the Nile*.

Pharaoh Senefru, or Snefru, ruled Egypt about 4,500 years ago. Senefru is famous for building the first of the great pyramids.